AWESOME AUTHORS

Edited By Holly Sheppard

First published in Great Britain in 2020 by:

Young Writers
Remus House
Coltsfoot Drive
Peterborough
PE2 9BF
Telephone: 01733 890066
Website: www.youngwriters.co.uk

Printed and bound in the UK by BookPrintingUK
Website: www.bookprintinguk.com
YB0439J

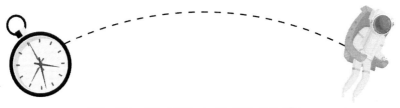

FOREWORD

Welcome, Reader!

Are you ready to enter the Adventure Zone? Then come right this way - your portal to endless new worlds awaits. It's very simple, all you have to do is turn the page and you'll be transported into a wealth of super stories.

Is it magic? Is it a trick? No! It's all down to the skill and imagination of primary school pupils from around the country. We gave them the task of writing a story on any topic, and to do it in just 100 words! I think you'll agree they've achieved that brilliantly – this book is jam-packed with exciting and thrilling tales.

These young authors have brought their ideas to life using only their words. This is the power of creativity and it gives us life too! Here at Young Writers we want to pass our love of the written word onto the next generation and what better way to do that than to celebrate their writing by publishing it in a book!

It sets their work free from homework books and notepads and puts it where it deserves to be – out in the world and preserved forever. Each awesome author in this book should be **super proud** of themselves, and now they've got proof of their ideas and their creativity in black and white, to look back on in years to come!

We hope you enjoy this book as much as we have. Now it's time to let imagination take control, so read on...

CONTENTS

Milecastle Primary School, Chapel House

Jessica Cheryl Rogers (11)	49
Ella Kaitlin Minto (10)	50
Iris Reid	51
Singe Ekwe (10)	52
Finley Dowson (11)	53
Curtis (10)	54
Lauren Burrows (10)	55
Jack Robinson (10)	56

North Lakes School, Penrith

Keian William McCombie (10)	57
Ava Grace Hodgson (10)	58
Megan Annette Gemmell (11)	59
Nathan Wardle (10)	60
Tabitha Payne (10)	61
Ronnie Hodgson (10)	62
Brooke Hettie Nugent (10)	63
Summer Eve Morrison (10)	64
Amy Snelson (10)	65
Whitney Armistead (9)	66
Emily Sandelands (10)	67
Dexter Kelly (10)	68
Caden James Harrison (11)	69
Henry Shane Allan (10)	70
Noah Robert Bowness (9)	71
Katie Richardson (9)	72
Oliver Cullen (9)	73
Rob Sisson (10)	74
Ellie-Mae Stephenson (10)	75
Alex Gill (9)	76
Elliott Dent (10)	77
Jayden Carr (9)	78
Lily Pluckrose (9)	79
Alessio Thompson (10)	80
Isobel Rose Simpson (10)	81
Reuben Tweddle (10)	82

Olga Primary School, Tower Hamlets

Labonnya Barua (9)	83
Mutahara Ahmed (7)	84
Evelyn Young (10)	85
Noah Brown (9)	86
Alisa Rahman (9)	87

Shirenewton Primary School, Shirenewton

Emma B	88
Chloe Hebblethwaite	89
Molly G	90
Kate	91
George Tom Lobb Siddall (9)	92
George S (9)	93
Caitlin Morgan (10)	94
Evan D	95
Ella Parnell (9)	96
Dylan Samuel Haddow (10)	97
Sienna Harford (11)	98
Zak Baker (9)	99
Evan Walker	100
Martha Evelyn Garrett Lupo (8)	101
Owen Read-Smith (9)	102
Alexander Duckworth (9)	103
Phoebe Hine (10)	104
Floelyn Lyra Skye Trim (10)	105
Megan (10)	106
Lauren Denné (9)	107
Isabel Bendall (9)	108
Terah Rose Parkhouse (10)	109
Ethan B	110
Seren Burston-Yates (9)	111
Demi Morgan	112
Aiden Carpenter	113
Evan F	114
Barnaby Hitchcock (10)	115
Thomas Burbidge (9)	116
Dylan Morgan Poole (10)	117

St Edward's RC Primary School, Lees

George Evans (10)	118
Bella Brennan (7)	119
Ellie-Beth Power (8)	120
Ciara Postlethwaite (10)	121
Eavan Malunga (10)	122
Yvonne Mwangi (10)	123
Amelia Grace Riley (7)	124
Carys Evans (9)	125
Rebecca Norton (10)	126
Annabelle Dervan (9)	127
Ella Barlow (9)	128
Alannah Ashton (8)	129
Sam Leach (10)	130
Emily Richmond (10)	131
Rory Nield (8)	132
Olly Maher (9)	133

St Joseph's Convent School For Girls, Wanstead

Jamie McKeith (9)	134
Samantha Sawyerr (7)	135
Maria Bedneau (8)	136
Zahra Nisar (8)	137
Olivia Day	138
Micheala Hagan (9)	139
Tiana John-Rose (8)	140
Maya Malik (9)	141
Anna Gillert (7)	142

Strathpeffer Primary School, Strathpeffer

Lewis Cameron King (10)	143
Grace Grant (10)	144
Harvey Wright (11)	145
Oona Macdonald (10)	146
Kayden Aird (10)	147
Lena Jean Butler-Whittaker (9)	148
Ieuan Hedges (10)	149
Charlotte Frame (10)	150

Charlotte Rose (9)	151
Cody Mackenzie (10)	152
Lara Maree Rasdale (10)	153
Ella Cormack (10)	154
Isla Stewart (10)	155
Fraser James Wright (11)	156
Teagen Syrjanen (10)	157
Fraser Alick Morrison (10)	158
Craig Stewart (10)	159
Katie Campbell (10)	160
Kai Condon (10)	161
Ali Taylor (9)	162

Wootton St Peter's CE Primary School, Wootton Village

Imogen Cobner-Vale (9)	163
Harriet Emily Johnson (10)	164
Rose Kyarra Stevens (9)	165
Bethany Rose (8)	166
Charlie Cooke (10)	167
Maria Catalina (7)	168
Ruby Gillett (9)	169

THE STORIES

TOP SECRET

My Brother Is Being Chased

Hi, my name is Alexander. I have a brother called Jayden. He was the best until this happened. As we were walking down the wet path, he asked me if I had seen his phone. Of course, I didn't know. When we got home, he told Mum that I had stolen his phone! I got told off. This happened every day for about a week. Then I saw it... A giant, black, winged creature! A demon! I told Mum. She didn't believe me. Every day this kept happening! I thought the demon was trying to kill my special brother, Jayden...

Melissa Kavak (11)
Anagh Coar Primary School, Anagh Coar

The Beautiful Rainforest Adventure!

One beautiful sunny and rainy day, Summer and her mother went out on an adventure into the wonderful rainforest. Whilst being on the train, they tried to spot some birds with their binoculars. Summer spotted ten beautiful blue tits. An hour later, they finally arrived so they started exploring the wonderful rainforest. Summer and her mother saw monkeys, frogs, snakes and slimy slugs! They saw the most beautiful thing they had ever seen. They saw all of the droplets falling off the green leaves on the trees and a wonderful rainbow! Then they sat and enjoyed the beautiful view.

Holly Cockings (8)
Bozeat Primary School, Bozeat

Out Of The Outskirts

Isaac and Kian headed to France when suddenly, the plane stopped and crashed! Isaac checked the adults' pulses. His uncle was dead and the pilot was stone cold! The boys checked for equipment. They were going to go on foot. They found a medic bag and a Bowie knife, then they set off! At night, they slept in a homemade shelter. When morning came, they climbed the mountains and descended into France, using their bags as sledges. They whizzed past bears and wolves to civilisation. When they got there, the boys just wanted food and to sleep in a bed.

Isaac James (8)
Bozeat Primary School, Bozeat

Hamster Bite

Once there lived a boy called Sam. He thought he had a special talent for football. One day, Sam was playing with his hamster.

"Sam?" his mum said.

"What?"

"You need to brush your hair!"

"One minute," said Sam.

Sam had never been bitten by his hamster but just then he got bitten by his hamster! Then he felt different. It felt like he was just saved. He went to the doctor and the doctor said, "It must have just been a fever."

At school, Sam then found out he had a special talent...

Kyle Douglass (7)
Bozeat Primary School, Bozeat

The Adventures Of Prue And The Gang!

Hi. I'm Alexa and I'm going to tell you the story of four kids who needed some help. They were named Prue, Piper, Page and Pheobe. They travelled to Magic Space. This was a faraway galaxy. This was not a place for butterflies and daisies. It was in fact, a superhero world! They got help from three superheroes named Bobby, Luke and Dave.
Boom! It went from problem to problem and Luke was gone! *Pop!* Luke was back and they were back in the town they lived in! They had so much fun.

Alexa Jessup (9)
Bozeat Primary School, Bozeat

The Upside-Down Universe

I heard a noise in the cupboard in the dead of night. I got out of bed and walked slowly towards the cupboard. I felt myself getting sucked in! A while later, I hit the ground a bit hard. It was very dark and I fainted. A while later, I woke up and loads of black, wet vines were all over me! A black goo appeared and saved me! I heard clicking and I got up and loads of bloodthirsty tarantulas chased me and zombies popped out of the ground! I found the cupboard and jumped back through...

Kyran Worrall (11)
Bozeat Primary School, Bozeat

There Is Something In My Room... Go And Run!

This may sound crazy but I think there's a ghost in my room. I've seen a figure at the end of my bunk bed but it's really blurry so I can't see its face. I'm starting to get really freaked out by it! It always comes at 3am sharp. I am only eight and I want to be left alone by this spirit at the end of my bed... My mother says that I'm not actually being visited by a ghost, I'm just seeing things. I know she's wrong. I'm going to find out about it...

Libby Stella Steel (11)
Bozeat Primary School, Bozeat

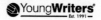

The Unicorn Princess

Unknowing of what I would find, I was falling through a sidewalk crack and I landed on a marshmallow. Also a queen's crown fell on my head! It was a candy crown. After a few days of being queen, I wandered around the candy forest and found a pink glowing egg in a tree! I needed to take it to Zanda to return it to her royalness, her mother, queen of all. She was an alicorn. She had lost her egg, an evil sorcerer stole it! She tried to defend the egg but she had failed to keep it.

Darla Goodes (10)
Bozeat Primary School, Bozeat

Scarlett Finds A Neon Unicorn In The Jungle

One day an explorer named Scarlett was in the jungle finding a neon unicorn. In the jungle she looked and looked until the found a piece of paper. It said 'To find me you need to find a cave that glows rainbow and there I'll be'. Scarlett couldn't wait to find the unicorn! She walked and walked until she found the cave that glowed rainbow. She was too excited! Then she found the neon unicorn! It glowed rainbow. She touched it and got superpowers and she had a very good life.

Scarlett Worrall (8)
Bozeat Primary School, Bozeat

The Adventure

Once upon a time there lived a girl called Alice and a dog called John. They lived at thirteen Queen Street and they had an older brother called Russell. Alice was ten years old and Russell was nineteen years old. Alice and John went out for a walk and they saw a black hole in front of them. They jumped into the hole at the same time! It took them to the year of the dinosaurs! They nearly got eaten by a dinosaur. Alice screamed. Then they went back home and played sketch it.

Ruby Cockings (7)
Bozeat Primary School, Bozeat

A Secret Chaser On The Case

One secret man was on the hunt because he stole something very secretive to the Prince of England. He would be found soon. Nobody should have been snooping around to get the item. Right now we were hunting the mystery man with the item down. The agents got the man and the mystery item back! The Prince of England needed the secretive item back... The prince is not himself without it...

Elouize Ellis (9)
Bozeat Primary School, Bozeat

Robo Ruckus

I was walking down the street when suddenly I got sucked into a portal! I had no idea where I was going. I felt strange. I looked at my hands and I knew I was a ninja! Then, *flash!* I saw a robot. I had a cool katana. I destroyed the robot and then more came! I looked in the distance and saw even more of them. I followed them and got to a castle. I snuck behind them. The castle was so big! Then I met their king... *Slash! Clang! Boom...*

Kylan Hadley (9)
Caslon Primary Community School, Halesowen

Impossible

Creak! Pugsley awoke. The small pug crept across the room searching for this mysterious noise. Through the princess-pink bedroom he went. Gliding through the sea of tiaras and fairy wings he went. Someone else was there! He heard something move on the shelf and when he looked up there was Bella the ballerina and Fluffy the teddy bear. *No - don't be so silly,* he told himself. Then Pugsley went to Jasper's room. But it was even more mysterious in there. The soldiers were riding dinosaurs! No, Milly and Jasper's toys did not move. Impossible! Or so he thought...

Amber Rowcliffe (9)
Chevening CE Primary School, Chipstead

The Halloween Letter

Seven-year-old Ben wasn't scared of much but when it was Halloween he got spooked at times, although he loved trick or treating with his friends. Ben was getting changed into his wizard costume when he suddenly heard a spooky noise coming from the wardrobe. What could it be? Ben tentatively opened his wardrobe door, heart racing. Searching slowly through his clothes, he could still hear the noise! Reaching to the back, Ben found a small envelope floating! Nervously, he opened it and gasped. It was an invitation to Hogwarts! Ben couldn't believe it. This was pure magic!

Lily Brooks (9)
Chevening CE Primary School, Chipstead

Pat Bat Gets Lost

There was once a bat called Pat. He went out one night for a fly and when he came back he couldn't remember which cave was his. So he went in the wrong one.

Three days later a boy came and found the little bat on the ground. He said, "Are you okay?"

"Yes. I'm just lost," Pat mumbled.

"Where do you live?" the boy asked.

"In a cave like this."

They travelled over the hills to another cave.

"Is this the cave?"

"Yes! Thanks," Pat said.

Pat flew into the dark cave and slept with his family happily.

Yvaine Pilcher (9)
Chevening CE Primary School, Chipstead

Sherbet

Once there was a girl named Ava who was tidying her room. Ava pulled out a toy box and fell in! Little did she know it was a portal to Candyland. Ava saw lollipop trees and candyfloss bushes. Wow! Suddenly, she saw mysterious footprints. She followed them.

Ava encountered a spotty-horned monster! It was scared as it was under attack by a candy factory gnome. It was up to Ava to save the monster. Ava pushed the gnome into a candyfloss bush where it became entangled in stickiness. Ava and the monster celebrated their victory by eating sherbet and lollipops.

Sophie Rimmer (9)
Chevening CE Primary School, Chipstead

The Code Room

The Allied Forces had just penetrated the German defence-line and were now invading Berlin. They were depending on decoding secret Nazi messages to find out their plans. Suddenly, in the message room an unknown reel of code transmitted through and caused the team to unsuccessfully try to decode it. Whilst all of that was happening, in the German General's room, Adolf Hitler was laughing over his plans to destroy the Allies with one nuclear strike! Back in the code room, they were jumping in joy. They knew the plans!
Boom! Germany was destroyed.

Matthew Wilde (9)
Chevening CE Primary School, Chipstead

Zoe's Magical Pet Discovery

For Zoe's tenth birthday she received a lovely snowy-white owl from her dad. He owned a pet shop just around the corner. Zoe named the owl Destiny because she thought the owl liked adventures. One evening she realised that Destiny was missing! She looked up and down the house but Destiny had disappeared. Zoe went to find her dad in the shop to see if the owl was there. To her surprise, there was a leopard staring into Zoe's eyes! The leopard looked strangely familiar because of the mark on its face. She'd seen it before...

Annabel Smith (9)

Chevening CE Primary School, Chipstead

Too Late To Turn Back

I rotated my globe. Suddenly, my world and I began to spin - faster, increasingly out of control! I had caused Planet Earth to travel forward in time to a time when a boiling sun scorched the ground, where islands were constantly under attack from surging waves, where glaciers melted into the sea and forests caught fire as quickly as striking a match! It was the world we had been warned about. A world damaged by humans, but now devoid of humans. In panic, I tried to reverse the globe but it was too late, the damage had been done.

Tristan Thompson (9)
Chevening CE Primary School, Chipstead

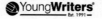

Unconscious

I woke up on a cold, crisp, dark morning. I looked out of the dusty window. The grass was covered in frost. I crept downstairs as quiet as a mouse, making sure I didn't wake anyone. As I made my way down the creaky corridor something caught my eye. In the distance was a bright, glistening, glowing light. I made my way to it but it was not what I thought it was; it was some sort of secret doorway. I hesitated then opened it. *Creak...* *Thump!* I hit the bottom. I awoke frightened but alive on my bedroom floor...

Eliza Mitchell (9)
Chevening CE Primary School, Chipstead

The Mystery Of Horror

Once there was a boy called Zack who hated his little sister Isla, who seemed to always have a dummy. Zack always went to school on time because he loved school. Now, let's get to the point. Zack had a strange thing about him... At night, his room would be silent and that's what was about to happen... dark, darker, darkest - silence. Then came a girl called Wednesday and her pet ghost Ghostie and a fanged unicorn. Little Wednesday scared Zack but was Wednesday really scary? She would prove him wrong, which she did. Confusingly.

Florence O'Brien (9)
Chevening CE Primary School, Chipstead

A Rip In Time

An ordinary man stepped through what he believed to be the door but turned out to be a rip in time! As he stepped, life drained out of him. He looked around with the final strength he had and saw a dark and desolate future - a thousand different dark and desolate futures. But there was one bright, shining future glowing in the darkness. The man grabbed hold of it with all his dying strength. Now he is cursed, like Atlas, to hold onto the bright future forever and ever, bound like a prisoner in chains - to save... us!

Adam Geer (9)

Chevening CE Primary School, Chipstead

The Rabbit's Great Escape!

Once there lived a family of bunnies who were living happily in a field. One day a farmer was shooting in their field. Suddenly, the man found the rabbits running around in his field! The farmer tried to shoot the rabbits but they managed to get away! They kept on running their fastest. Then they came to a secret land of fields that had a glass ball around the edge so that no one could get inside, unless they needed somewhere safe to go. They lived happily ever after there with a nice farmer. He fed them!

Sofia Devine (9)

Chevening CE Primary School, Chipstead

The Horrible Snowman

In a treacherous forest where a snowman lives and where he freezes people, a man called Jeffery was cutting down some trees. The snowman chased him out of the forest and he ran and ran until there was no sight of the snowman! The snowman went back to where he lived. Jeffrey called 999 and the police came to melt the snowman. The snowman ran into a policeman who pulled out a hairdryer and turned it on! Melt, melt, melt. He dissolved into nothing and so Jeffrey saved the day! Chop, chop, chop... or did he?

Samuel Wilding (10)
Chevening CE Primary School, Chipstead

The Mystery Of Paper Bag Boy

Long ago in a peaceful town, a boy named Kwebukop smothered a man into the woods nearby and threw a paper bag and poison at him! The man spluttered and coughed. He turned into Paper Bag Boy. Kwebukop fled out of the woods. Paper Bag Boy hunted down Kwebukop. He chased him out of town into a tunnel and he ran and ran like a cheetah! Soon enough, Kwebukop ran out of breath. Paper Bag Boy held him up and choked him to death. From that day onwards, he was feared throughout the town's existence.

Sebastian Murphy (10)
Chevening CE Primary School, Chipstead

Life On Mars

Hi, I'm Max and I live on Mars. You see, I was taken by some creature. Well, here's the story of how I got here...

I was working in Area 51 one night when suddenly a huge light came crashing down near one of the buildings! I ran over there and walked into the building. There was nothing there so I decided to walk out. Then I saw a flying thing! I was blown over by the wind but then I ran. The flying thing followed me until I started to fly! Then I just woke up on Mars!

Kit Hodson (10)

Chevening CE Primary School, Chipstead

Murderer's Revenge

I am dead. I am a murderer's soul. I loved, I have had love betrayed. I have taken my revenge - twice. I loved more than any man, born into this world to love. Then she betrayed me. My heart's desire betrayed me. She loved another. Darkness took over my heart. I killed her. I was punished for that action. I was killed for that moment. My death came in the form of revenge, revenge upon her murderer - revenge from her first lover. I was killed. I killed myself.

James Wood (10)
Chevening CE Primary School, Chipstead

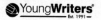
Ghost World

Millie was walking through a graveyard when she tripped. However, the pain she had expected did not come, instead her body met a strange substance like water but changed! It was her street. There was her house but something was different... Everything was greyer than usual, the lampposts, the houses, and nothing looked solid. There were people gliding eerily along the street! Millie walked towards one of them and her curiosity got the better of her. She touched one. Millie's hand went straight through it! Ghosts? The world was full of ghosts? Where on Earth was she?

Florence Ashton (8)

Finton House School, Wandsworth

The Detective

Once there was a detective called Mr Frost. He was on an investigation to find a missing child called Lucy. Mr Frost wasn't a very good detective. "Lucy!" he cried. "Lucy, come here!"
Mr Frost knew that if he found Lucy, he would get a £50,000 reward.
"I'm here!" said a loud voice behind him.
Mr Frost turned around and he saw a shadow lurking in the darkness. He saw a little girl. "Arghh! Are you..." cried Mr Frost.
"Lucy, yes! Can you help me find my parents?" asked Lucy.
Yes! £50,000 here I come, thought Mr Frost.

Mathilda Uttley (8)
Finton House School, Wandsworth

The Amazing Accusation

It was August 1928. Mr James was lured into the head office. His heart was pounding as he entered the sleek room. "Sit!" the man exclaimed, beckoning him closer. Agent James moved closer cautiously to the peculiar man. All of a sudden, he heard something coming from the room upstairs. Now he was anxious. Why was he in here? What had he done? How? When did he do it? Agent James soon because suspicious; his shoulders tightened, his lips became dry and his breath cold. "So, Agent James, I hear you've become a double agent!"
James gasped, aghast...

Seva Ruparel (9)
Finton House School, Wandsworth

Alien On Earth

The glowing green alien swooped through the black hole, wondering what he'd find, when he glimpsed something deadly... Earth! He found himself hurtling towards the hard tiles of a human roof. He landed on a chimney and fell down towards a boiling pot! Realising that his jetpack didn't work, he nimbly swung over the pot's edge. He saw a huge creature passing by. It had four legs but it was only standing on two! Its face was a slightly pink colour and it was shouting horribly loudly. He looked up. This one was going to take a lot of skill...

Alexander Petecki (9)
Finton House School, Wandsworth

The Creature

I lay in the cool, dark room. The trees whispered to each other and the twigs cracked in greeting. I felt oblivious to the intriguing conversation nature was making. I envied the normal world, cut off from any trouble at all. Anyway, I was lying in bed when I heard a strange noise. A queer cry, a lost call. I was so interested by this, it was a toe-curling twist to my traumatic tale. I snuck out of bed and peered into the eerie glow. Suddenly, the floaty mist surrounding the woods disappeared and I saw the strangest creatures, *Unicorn-cats!?*

Christabel Mary Alice Fletcher (9)
Finton House School, Wandsworth

The Day My Toys Came Alive

As I woke up, my eyes adjusted to the morning sun. I got a creeping suspicion this was not going to be a normal day. Suddenly I spotted a sight that had never been seen before! My doll was crawling over to my bed! As I looked over at my toy cupboard, I saw a scene of chaos. Toys walking, talking, playing and going to school! It was a surprising sight as my doll was moving. I averted my eyes only to see my teddy bear, Dexter, choosing clothes from the doll's house! I was more surprised than ever before.

Grace Howson (8)
Finton House School, Wandsworth

The Lion And The Hydra

I raced towards the portal as the ravenous Hydra snapped at me. I tore towards the portal but at that moment, the Hydra pounced! It landed on my leg and I felt an agonising crack as it broke in two. At that moment, the Nemean lion appeared out of thin air and simultaneously bit off the Hydra's foot! It put me onto its back, streaking towards the portal like a budgie from a hawk rather than a mythical lion from a Hydra. I held on for dear life as I was catapulted back into my bed in the real world!

George Hufton (10)
Finton House School, Wandsworth

Katie's Adventure

It was Saturday. Katie jumped out of bed, so excited for the day ahead. She had planned to go to the park with her friend Lucy. "Bye, Mum!" Katie shouted as she slammed the door. When Katie and Lucy got to the park they noticed something was different. At the bottom of the park they saw some twinkling in the distance! "What could it be?" whispered Lucy.

"Let's go and investigate," said Katie.

When they got down to the twinkles they discovered it was a lake. Katie looked into the lake. This was no ordinary lake, she saw the future...

Lily Menzies (8)
Heathfield School, Rishworth

The Fight Of Powerland

In Powerland there was a mighty god called Ben Zeno. A clone called Neb Onez was plotting to overthrow him. Neb Onez had found the secret portal to Powerland and was gathering an army for the assault! Once through the portal, they gained the Powerland blessing, increasing their power by 1,000 times. Neb Onez's power rival, Ben Zeno, and the citizens of Powerland fought back. They were successful against the army, but Neb Onez was too powerful! Ben joined the battle with his two swords of light. It was a close battle, but good. They triumphed and balance was restored!

Ben Alexander Lacy (8)
Heathfield School, Rishworth

Alien Martians Destroy The Universe

Once on Planet Earth, there lived a mad chemist called Dr Snoopleface. Dr Snoopleface was so mad, the president made him do his job. One day, some aliens came to Planet Earth! Dr Snoopleface shouted because he was made to say, "Us humans declare peace."

But the aliens shouted back, "We do not want peace, we want to destroy your universe."

One by one the planets in our universe disappeared! Right now the human race was disappearing into space. The aliens ruled the whole universe! It turned out that Dr Snoopleface was an alien. He never did his job properly.

Agatha Wint (9)
Heathfield School, Rishworth

What's The Answer?

Ellie wanted to know the answers. She asked her parents, it was no good. She would never find the answer! She would travel anywhere! So one dark quiet night she crept into the Queen's palace! She whispered to the Queen her question. She didn't know either! She packed her bags to travel 1,000,000 miles into space! She was petrified! She saw an alien! Eeek! As she calmed down she asked her big, big, question. The alien replied, *beeep!* She asked the Earth too! She travelled the world. She asked the sea and sky. She found the answer finally... Google it!

Holly Menzies (8)
Heathfield School, Rishworth

Super Derek

Derek walked sleepily into his wardrobe and right out through the back. People were screaming and running. Loose Trousers had returned to wreck the village of Revilo. His legs were happily walking towards Loose Trousers, and he couldn't seem to control his feet. His heart was beating so quickly he was sure Loose Trousers could hear it. Then the words started... Derek couldn't control those either! Whatever he said worked because Loose Trousers ran faster than anything Derek had seen before. *What a dream*, Derek thought as he woke in shock.

Oliver Oates (8)
Heathfield School, Rishworth

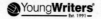
Teleportation Tale

Yesterday I was walking through the woods when I stepped on a twig and suddenly there were colours all around me swirling down to the floor. I was teleported to a cave! As I touched the walls, glowing fireflies were hovering before me. That didn't matter. Where was I? In the sky? Underground? Under the sea? I wandered further into the cave as the fireflies lit the way. Slowly they drifted out of sight. A shiver ran down my spine! Out of the darkness came two figures with blood-red eyes, shining brightly. I stammered, "Hello, who are you?"

Beatrice Blincoe (8)
Heathfield School, Rishworth

The Stolen Jewel

Once there was a museum and there was a precious jewel. The cleaner stole it! The next day the curator came to the museum. The gem was stolen and he panicked and told Detective Zoe. She called the police who arrived straight away. The police got the CCTV footage to confirm it was the cleaner. They stayed overnight to capture the culprit. They got the cleaner's bin bag and looked inside to find the precious turquoise jewel and other things like wallets, necklaces, earrings and gold blocks! The cleaner was taken to the police station and got arrested.

James Heptonstall (8)
Heathfield School, Rishworth

Jeff Chungers And The Golden Glove

Once upon a time on a rock of invisibility a boy called Jeff Chungers and his grandma Sassy Susan, lived in the mansion of royalty. Jeff and Susan went down to the mysterious cave under the mansion. Then Jeff saw a golden glove with some sort of diamonds in it! Then he put the gold and shiny glove on.

"Susan, please let me out of this glove... Cool, I've got superpowers now! I can fight Mr Fatty Johnathan Ripples. There he is, look! Susan, you can stay here while I fight."

That's what you get, Mr Fatty Johnathan Ripples...

Cahal Cooney (8)
Heathfield School, Rishworth

A Mystery Machine

A long time ago there was a girl named Zoe and she was a detective. Every early morning and night she would go outside quickly and fly around on her unicorn, Emerald, and see if there was any trouble around. One day Zoe saw Doctor Frufrufuffle working on a new machine. So Zoe and Emerald flew down to see what was going on. To their surprise, they saw a purple unicorn coming out of the machine! Zoe and Emerald were shocked because Doctor Frufrufuffle's machines never worked! Doctor Frufrufufuffle was happy. It was Zoe's job to stop her...

Isabelle Florence Gray (8)
Heathfield School, Rishworth

The Purr-Fect Adventure

One morning I walked downstairs and noticed the front door was wide open. I was scared because the kittens were not in my house. Me and mummy ran outside and saw a trail leading to the forest. We both jumped on my magic scooter to rescue the kittens. In the forests we heard scary meows then saw a gorilla carrying the poor kittens! Mummy pushed the magic button on my scooter and we began to fly. The gorilla was so shocked that he dropped the kittens! This gave us the chance to quickly scoop them up to safety and back home.

Scarlett Buckley (8)
Heathfield School, Rishworth

Super Bob Saves The World

Once upon a time there was a superhero called Super Bob. His superpowers were to teleport, also flying and turning himself invisible. He could also save the entire universe. Once he flew across a deep jungle and he saw a crocodile chasing a baby gorilla. *Snap, snap!* The little baby gorilla got chased up a tree. Luckily the gorilla had a banana peel and it threw the banana peel into the crocodile's mouth! Then Super Bob blasted in and he saved the baby gorilla by turning invisible and pinching the crocodile.

Ben Remmers (8)
Heathfield School, Rishworth

Asterea

Once upon a time, there was a girl called Asterea. Her uncle was a mean and evil scientist called Marc. Asterea hated Marc so much she left him. She went on a yak to a desert island but her boat broke! Luckily she ended up on the beach. She found a monkey and a parrot. She loved them so much.

The next day she went into the jungle and met another person, it was her long-lost sister! Together they found a treasure chest. It was filled with gold so they didn't need to worry about money ever again.

Isla Turner (8)
Heathfield School, Rishworth

Emma And The Magical World

I was at my grandma's house eating chocolate when I noticed a crack in the wall. I put my head in it and wriggled through it like a worm. I saw a bubble and had to jump through it! I fell onto a magnificent animal. I looked all around me. It was truly incredible! The animal landed and a little girl ran to me and said happily, "Hi! Would you like to come to our amazing party?"

I said, "Y-Y-Yes! What food is there?"

She said, "There are turkeys and fudge and pears and we dance all night!"

Connie Wood (8)
Heathfield School, Rishworth

One Young Cutlery Boy

Once there was a boy in a school dining room eating his lunch. His name was Daniel. He was eating his favourite food, pizza, and then he noticed that nobody was using their knife and fork properly. He was upset by their rude manners and so he got the knives and forks in his hands and made a change to all this madness! He realised he had powers to summon knives and forks to himself! Once he was in the park and the Justice Getters saw him with his amazing powers, they wanted to put him on their team.

Thomas Miller (9)
Heathfield School, Rishworth

A Battle Of Unhuman Beings

The dead forest was silent. On the north side were vampires and on the south side were werewolves! At midnight, the arch-enemy teams commenced battle, carrying pitchforks. Venomous fangs against piercing claws. The teams battled, attacking each other. After two long hours, most of the courageous warriors had been defeated! The final three remained: two werewolves and one vampire. One werewolf angrily stabbed the vampire! The vampire viciously bit him on the wrist! At exactly the same moment, they fell to the ground. Thunder roared ferociously. The final being was a hybrid of both! All was peaceful.

Jessica Cheryl Rogers (11)
Milecastle Primary School, Chapel House

The Sudden Regret

Lucy finally arrived at her camping spot. Gazing at the midnight sky, she discovered a full moon. She went to lean on the biggest tree. Being interrupted by glancing at the sky, she heard a ridiculously loud *creak*. Lucy fell unexpectedly into what seemed to be a tree! Landing on her head, she got up and walked across the room. Glaring at some stairs, her legs uncontrollably started approaching them! She found a room with diamond walls! She completed the final task of matching the puzzles and she arrived back at camping! Or so she thought. It wasn't done yet...

Ella Kaitlin Minto (10)

Milecastle Primary School, Chapel House

50

The Attic

What was it? The sound was so intriguing, she had to look. As quietly as possible, she opened the door. Everything was pitch-black. At first, she thought it was the usual lighting of the attic but then she realised it wasn't the attic, it was an open black space! When her eyes adjusted to the abyss of darkness, she noticed an ominous figure in front of her. It began to talk and all she heard was 'beware' before everything disappeared. The next thing she knew, she was on the floor surrounded by her distraught parents and her worried family...

Iris Reid
Milecastle Primary School, Chapel House

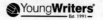
A Battle Between Heavenly Spirits

Deep in what I thought was a normal forest, I knew at that moment I was wrong. This forest had never been searched and I was about to be the first. This dusty path seemed endless. Every step I took, my heart beat faster. I was shaking controllably. Were my eyes deceiving me or had I caught a glimpse of something deep in the forest? One thing led to another and I saw an evil devil and a godly goddess battling! As darkness cast its eerie shadow, this place seemed scary, sinister and uninviting. *I'll make it alive*, I thought...

Singe Ekwe (10)
Milecastle Primary School, Chapel House

Alex And The Aliens

In a populated city cars flew over buildings. Everything was normal until aliens flew over the city, abducting everyone in sight! Alex was being chased, running faster than a cheetah. He led them towards the desert. He let them capture him because he had a cunning plan! Alex was in a cell with others from his city. He told everyone his plan so they cut a hole in the bars, found the control room and they went to start fighting! The aliens had no weapons so they backed down. After this, Alex was known as a hero.

Finley Dowson (11)
Milecastle Primary School, Chapel House

Death Watch

My name is Shero. I ventured to a black hole. Luckily I managed to survive the gravitational pull somehow. I managed to travel to the future and I could not believe my eyes! I met an old wrinkly man who was selling symbiotes. I bought a symbiote and it allowed me to control time, alter reality, break reality and teleport! I went back to the black hole and dark matter consumed me. I knew it would be the end... The dark matter turned my eyes black and my hands into massive talons with nails! Now I am Kronos...

Curtis (10)

Milecastle Primary School, Chapel House

The Hunt For A Missing Girl

In an abandoned jungle there was a nine-year-old girl who had been missing for a week. There were people looking for her ever since she went missing. She had been on the news four times and still no one had found her! There were people still out there today. They tried their very best to try and find her in the abandoned jungle. People said it was impossible to try and find her. Then they used helicopters and search dogs! After a long day of trying to find her, a hero finally found her!

Lauren Burrows (10)
Milecastle Primary School, Chapel House

Jack's Journey

Deep in what I thought was the jungle, I stood in fear, waiting for something to come. Suddenly, out came a unicorn with a dog! I was scared at first but they went the other way. They were leading me to a colossal door. The door was open. They both walked in. I followed. I was too scared not to. The path went on and on and on, it was never-ending. Suddenly the path came to an abrupt end. I heard the door creak loudly. I ran and ran. The door shut. I was trapped! I was so scared...

Jack Robinson (10)
Milecastle Primary School, Chapel House

The End Of Humanity

As Richie and the police landed on Salvort, the pressure began to build. They were here because of man-eating Dingo. As Richie stepped on Salvort, toothed suns and giant rock spines greeted them. They needed to eliminate Dingo or else they were doomed! Suddenly, Dingo shot from behind a rock and bellowed in hunger. Dingo approached a colleague and ate him! Screams filled Salvort as the officer cut Dingo while he was mutated. Richie thought he was dead. He was wrong. The monster scuttled over and then somehow disappeared... Celebrating, a shadow then loomed over Richie! Then everything went black...

Keian William McCombie (10)
North Lakes School, Penrith

The Magical Myth

It was midday. The tide was coming in, and fast! She shivered. Ocean needed to know why strange things kept happening at the beach before anyone got injured. Then she found an ocean-blue portal which she strode through! Everything looked magical in this new world. All the enchanted and wonderful creatures from myths were there! Suddenly, everything fell silent. The creatures speedily dashed away and out of nowhere, a beast appeared! Ocean made it disappear. She saved the legends! When Ocean returned, the beach was calm, beautiful and peaceful. She had done it! It was safe and protected forever.

Ava Grace Hodgson (10)
North Lakes School, Penrith

Two Hidden Doors

In a gloomy forest, there were some friends and they loved going on mysteries and adventures. They gathered in the park. They arrived at the park. Annie whispered to her friends, "We'll find something to explore!"

Later, Joy exclaimed, "Forest!"

All of them went into the creepy forest. The branches were broken, the soggy leaves lying on the floor in a heap. Suddenly, Jack had a thought. They decided to go but slowed down, the fog was hitting. As they got closer, the friends were terrified. Then they saw two enormous doors! Would they choose the right door...

Megan Annette Gemmell (11)
North Lakes School, Penrith

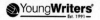

Quokka Island

It just took one discarded cigarette. Within minutes, the flames started flickering and rising! The dry grass turned bright orange as the dangerous fire started to spread quickly. Firefighters had landed on tiny Rottnest Island with long hoses and firefighting equipment. There was no time to spare, the rare animals on the island needed saving. A group of teddy bear faces with brown fur and little round ears and noses started to appear from under the trees! One by one they started quickly hopping towards the firefighters who couldn't believe their eyes. Quokkas really did exist!

Nathan Wardle (10)
North Lakes School, Penrith

Freya The Centaur

It's my trial today! I gasped. As the blazing sun roared through the afternoon, I grew anxious. The willow trees seemed to understand me and slumped. I was late! I galloped towards the jungle. My elder brother had done it before and he said, "It should be fine!"
As I stepped in, I felt the humid air travelling through the trees. A few hours later, I had found shelter. *Roar!* What was that? I fell asleep after a short amount of time.
When I woke up, I realised I was still in my bed! "I am Freya the centaur!"

Tabitha Payne (10)
North Lakes School, Penrith

A Spectacular Trip!

As Steve, Alex and Bob strolled through the luscious emerald field, the bright clear sky's heavens opened. They were going to find a cure for Alex's severe nausea. Suddenly a bright glow appeared. Jedi! One, two... eight! How would they fight? What on Earth could they possibly do? As the foe charged forward, they had to. Men were falling fast, in their favour! *Chop!* The last man down. They had won the fatal battle and taken down some of the most iconic Jedi! Now though it was time to find the cure, as that was their ambition for the journey...

Ronnie Hodgson (10)
North Lakes School, Penrith

Jumanji Slayers

Long ago lived two boys. Their names were Ethan and Kaine. Both were very smart. Ethan always planned the missions but Kaine was the person to do the missions. One day the two played a game of Jumanji. Both were transported to another dimension! They landed in a cave full of deadly vipers. After eighteen hours, both boys had slain horrid vipers. They were so close to the end but all of a sudden, a colossal spider climbed down from its snowy-white web! Both of the boys charged. *Smack! Boom! Bang!* The monster of Jumanji was no more...

Brooke Hettie Nugent (10)
North Lakes School, Penrith

My Crazy Journey To The 4000s

Emerging from the shadows was a shining portal! I curiously trudged into it. I looked around. The land was dry, dark and lonely. I needed out. Two hours later I finally saw some nearby citizens and questioned them where I was exactly. They responded with, "England!" It was Tuesday the third of October in the year 4000. I was 1980 years into the future! I sprinted. I finally found an exit out of this dark, derelict, dry land. It was my only choice to leave! I got back home and I learned to never go through random portals again.

Summer Eve Morrison (10)
North Lakes School, Penrith

Polly The Panther

As I walked through the glistening, shimmering rainforest, there was nobody to be seen. Normally Tilly the tiger would shout my name if she ever needed help. In a blink of an eye, Tilly shouted my name like she was in trouble! Then I realised with every step I took, my paws were getting hotter and hotter. Suddenly I found out the forest was on fire! It was spreading like wildfire. As fast as a cheetah, the fire got worse and worse. Then Tilly came out with everyone! Without warning, the fire spread more, endangering all the animals...

Amy Snelson (10)
North Lakes School, Penrith

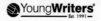

Jumanji!

Whitney and her brother were playing Jumanji the board game.
"Six, well done Leon!" said Whitney.
Then the ground began to shake.
"What is happening?" screamed Leon.
"I don't know!" shouted Whitney.
A giant whirlpool appeared and sucked them both up! When they were in the place, they had to finish the game. Whitney had to roll a ten. "Ten!" screamed Whitney. The portal was back. Suddenly, a hippo jumped in along with them! Back at home, they sat with their parents.
"We love you!" said Whitney and Leon.

Whitney Armistead (9)
North Lakes School, Penrith

The Mystery Monster

Tom Granty was in a forest. He was looking for a mysterious creature which had never been found. Tom was a very tall man with a skinny body. He was a spy. His large feet crunched into the snow hill. In a blink, Tom heard something between the trees. He looked around and saw a purple-bluey slimy monster! It had eight legs and no arms. He stepped towards the monster and scooped it home! Finally, he found out if he really was the creature he was looking for. The monster invaded the city and took precious things from people's homes...

Emily Sandelands (10)
North Lakes School, Penrith

Billy The Pig

Billy the pig dreamt of having wings and a lightsaber. Billy came bouncing outside and woke everyone up. They were fuming. The farmer gave Billy a belly rub. When he woke up, Billy had wings and a glowing lightsaber! Then there was a scream. There was a ship and Norris was carrying Baby Yoda! Then the ship set off. Billy flew to space and boarded the ship! Baby Yoda was tied up and Billy took out his lightsaber and made a portal and kicked Norris away. Billy grabbed Baby Yoda and took him back safely. Then they started to sing.

Dexter Kelly (10)
North Lakes School, Penrith

The Saviour Of Slendor

As Ben, a scientist, entered space, he was about to puncture into the solar system. Quickly, he looked up. A whole new galaxy was upon him! He got closer to a planet and it looked like it was in trouble, even from a thousand miles. He rushed down as fast as he could. Ben was told they were being raided, so he swung his invention, the laser blade, and started slaying! After he went a bit too overboard, the planet thanked him for saving the universe. The government of Slendor crowned Ben king and saviour to all!

Caden James Harrison (11)
North Lakes School, Penrith

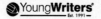

The Second Player

In his worn-out attic, Michael decided to play Uno. He went to get the cards out, the reverse card wasn't there. In its place, there was a glowing alien card. He grabbed it and... *poof!* He became an alien! His tongue was two metres long and he had acid breath. Something wasn't right. He still had to find a second player! Instead he found a UFO and hopped in. Then he saw that they had the second player trapped! How could he get past them? He had no clue... Soon he woke up! Was it a dream?

Henry Shane Allan (10)
North Lakes School, Penrith

Sydney In Danger!

John had woken up to the vibrating of his phone. The CNN news had popped up! He read it. It said 'Bush fires on the edge of Sydney'. Then John realised that he lived on the side of Sydney! He rushed out of bed and packed some food and clothes. He zoomed out of his house to the coast of Sydney to get a boat. The mass machine zoomed across the pier and splashed into the water! John checked his phone and saw the fire tearing through his garden. A tear trickled down his cheek as the fire burned.

Noah Robert Bowness (9)
North Lakes School, Penrith

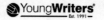

The Australian Outback

Once I went to the Australian Outback but there was a smoky smell. I heard something scuttling... There it was again! Suddenly two bearded dragons popped out! One was a baby one and a mummy one with ninety-eight more behind them, shaking with fear! I looked up and saw tonnes of smoke. I needed to get them out of here. Luckily I had my suitcase so I opened it up and put most of them in! I carried the rest. I rushed to a river but there was a fire in the way... Eventually, we got there safely.

Katie Richardson (9)
North Lakes School, Penrith

The Alien That Loved Halloween

One weird Halloween night, the sky was covered by clouds. As the clocks struck midnight, a bright light pierced through the darkness as a space shuttle crashed with a thud! Moments later, a green, slimy creature emerged from the depths of the spacecraft and floated towards the smell of leftover Halloween treats. Then the alien turned invisible and entered the houses. Before you could say the words 'trick or treat', all of the chocolates had vanished for another Halloween...

Oliver Cullen (9)
North Lakes School, Penrith

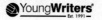
Bob The Time Traveller

As the pod rumbled, Bob (a time traveller) held on for dear life. When he got there, he was at a Roman camp in 407 AD. He hid by the trees to watch the fight between Rome and Britannia which was tomorrow. Bob had been awoken to hear the British were there. Roman soldiers headed towards them! Britain started to charge, although they kept calm to take them down! Time passed. Bob was still watching and the Romans had won! Many soldiers were dead and a great leader of Rome sadly died.

Rob Sisson (10)
North Lakes School, Penrith

The Dragon Who Saves The World

Ellie mysteriously heard an explosion from a distance away. Ellie dashed as fast as she could and went towards the explosion. Shockingly, Ellie saw a nice dragon and an evil and disrespectful dragon! The evil dragon was trying to destroy the world by making fires! Ellie saw the good dragon stopping the evil dragon from making fire by pouring freezing cold water on him! The evil dragon squealed and disintegrated into ash before Ellie's eyes. The good dragon had saved the world!

Ellie-Mae Stephenson (10)
North Lakes School, Penrith

Deep-Sea Diving

The deep-sea diver felt as if it was his first-ever dive. He had never dived in this part of the ocean but as well as being anxious, he was excited! This time he had a new diving suit which would take him to greater depths. All around him were scuttling fish. He felt at home there. The deeper he got, the darker it got. In the distance, he could see something amazing. Something out of the ordinary. A hidden city! This would be his greatest discovery yet...

Alex Gill (9)
North Lakes School, Penrith

The Ghostly Dreamy

One day at school, all of my friends were saying ghosts were real. They dared me to go to an abandoned house the following week. The day came and as I walked up to the front door, I was dripping with sweat. The door creaked open so in I went, avoiding all of the cobwebs hanging down! The door banged shut behind me so I ran to the corner and closed my eyes. I slowly opened my eyes after a minute and realised I was in my own bed! It was all just a dream.

Elliott Dent (10)
North Lakes School, Penrith

Blobby The Mythical Monster

A long time ago in a land no human would think of, there was an unknown species called The Blobby. It was a magical creature. They had their own ways of doing everything but there was one Blobby that did things differently. He went out hunting on his own. Everyone always questioned him about it. He never used to reply. One day he went into the forest and saw a flickering flame and noticed that it was a fire! Then they all went to put the fire out.

Jayden Carr (9)
North Lakes School, Penrith

Lily And The Dragon

At the beginning, Lily Potter got her acceptance letter to tell her she had a place at Hogwarts School of Witchcraft and Wizardry! Later at the sorting celebration, Lily was sorted into Hufflepuff. The next morning she went down to breakfast and heard squealing coming from the broom shed. Lily felt curious. She had a peek in the broom shed and found a Swedish Short Snout! After weeks of training, Lily set the dragon free.

Lily Pluckrose (9)
North Lakes School, Penrith

Odd Dogs

I opened my eyes to the sound of what I thought was a dog peeking through the gap in the curtains. I was not expecting what I saw. It was a very small dog with wings and a horn floating one metre above the ground! My eyes almost popped out of my tiny head. Over to my left dressed in a bun costume was a sausage dog, then a dog casually pushing a puppy in a stroller! This must have been the odd dog realm...

Alessio Thompson (10)
North Lakes School, Penrith

Animal Land

I stepped through a vibrant portal, not knowing what dangers lurked inside. After my eyes straightened, I looked across the landscape and saw a mirror. I looked into it and saw a new me... I was different. There was a cat on a tree swing and a lion on a lead like it was on a walk! "This is a weird land..." I said.

Isobel Rose Simpson (10)
North Lakes School, Penrith

Australian Bush Fires

One hot, sunny day in Australia I was driving down the never-ending highway but suddenly, in the corner of my eye, I saw a poor koala stuck in a tree that was on fire! So I pulled over and jumped over the barrier and tugged the koala so it was safe. Then I took it to the doctor.

Reuben Tweddle (10)
North Lakes School, Penrith

The Nine Deaths

One day a girl Jennie was home alone. Her mother worked and Jennie was hungry. She went to the kitchen for snacks. However, when leaving her bedroom, the door slammed, hitting her. When Jennie felt blood, she cried in agony, then passed out while hearing a woman giggle... She heard the giggle eight times. When she passed out with the giggle, then everything would go back to normal. Jennie told her mother. She explained that she would die when she heard the screams for the ninth time. After Jennie's birthday, she prayed that she wouldn't face the ninth death scream...

Labonnya Barua (9)
Olga Primary School, Tower Hamlets

The Lost Unicorn

In a faraway land, there was an enchanted forest. A fairy kingdom was deep inside. A magical unicorn named Skyler was the protector of the kingdom. There was a wicked fairy who also lived amongst them. The unicorn was loyal to her king but deep inside her heart, she felt empty.
One starry night, Skyler had enough. In desperation, she ran away into the deep woods! "Here I come, freedom!" she exclaimed joyfully. Out of nowhere, she was captured by the evil fairy! Suddenly, the king found out that Skyler was missing! Could he save Skyler or not?

Mutahara Ahmed (7)
Olga Primary School, Tower Hamlets

What Was That?

As I was playing with my Lego, my busy mum shouted, "Dinner!"

When I turned around, out of the corner of my eye I saw something move. We didn't have a dog or cat, Mum said it would ruin our furniture. I don't agree. Anyway, I turned again and saw my Lego actually moving! "Hello?" I whispered. "Can you hear me?"

My Lego's pale expressions seemed surprised. They hadn't realised I was there.

"You coming?" my mum called.

"Yes, Mum!" and as I walked further and further away, I heard their faint voices trailing off...

Evelyn Young (10)
Olga Primary School, Tower Hamlets

Trick Or Treat?

It was Halloween. Chloe was out trick or treating. Across the street, she saw an old house. Its walls were black and among the bushes, there was a pumpkin lit with a candle. She knocked on the ancient door. As it creaked open, a bony skeleton hand pulled Chloe in! She screamed and tried to run away but she was trapped! Then the lights flicked on and it was a boy doing a stupid trick. She walked away, relieved. Then she felt like someone or something was following her. "Trick or treat, Chloe?" said a real bony skeleton behind her...

Noah Brown (9)
Olga Primary School, Tower Hamlets

The Story Of Royals

Once there lived a queen who was going to give birth. The king really wanted to know if it was a boy or girl, so the king's sorcerer and the queen's nanny came downstairs to tell the king. They checked with a scan. "It's twins!" they said.
The king was so shocked but the king and queen felt danger, so they gave one baby to the sorcerer and one to the nanny. They both took them far away from the palace. The king and queen sadly died! The nanny, the sorcerer and the little baby girls were safe and protected.

Alisa Rahman (9)
Olga Primary School, Tower Hamlets

Rudolph's Adventure!

Once there was a reindeer called Rudolph who slept in a park near the North Pole, abandoned by a mean girl called Ezmerelda. One Christmas Eve, Santa noticed little Rudolph and took him in his sleigh. Once all the presents were delivered, Santa took Rudolph to his grotto.

"What's your name?"

"R-Rudolph," he said nervously.

"Well have a cookie," said Santa.

He grew up with Santa, but one day everything changed. Ezmerelda burst through the door! Rudolph and Santa tried to fight her but failed. Then Rudolph's nose started to glow and Ezmerelda fell to the ground into dust!

Emma B

Shirenewton Primary School, Shirenewton

Rainbow The Magic Unicorn

Rainbow invited her friends over to play because it was her birthday party. She had invited her friends Sparkle, Dasher, Glitter and Wonder. She was Rainbow the magic unicorn. She came home from the park to a sticky slimy birthday party. When she got home, her friends were not there like they had planned! Rainbow looked all over. She couldn't actually think her friends would have done that to her... "Surprise!" all her friends shouted. "We hid! Happy birthday!"
Rainbow was so happy. For her birthday, she got some rainbow glitter dust hoof polish and the best birthday party ever.

Chloe Hebblethwaite
Shirenewton Primary School, Shirenewton

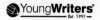

Food Adventure!

Once there was an alien who always went on different adventures. Today he went to Food Land. "Wow!" said the alien. The alien kept on walking until eventually, he found someone... or something! He found a potato which was alive!
"Hello," said the potato. "Come with me."
The potato and the alien were walking along until they saw a huge bin. The potato chucked the alien in!
"Ahhh," said the alien. "Ewww!"
There was so much waste and food but there was also a door that led his way home at last! Always recycle, don't just throw it away!

Molly G
Shirenewton Primary School, Shirenewton

Late Night Murders

One cold, dark November night, Cassandra Millers is out for a late-night walk around the village of Shirenewton. Cassandra turns into the churchyard to conclude her walk when she feels someone breathing down her neck. She turns in shock to see her friend May Wood standing behind her. "May!" says Cassandra in shock and horror. To her surprise, May takes her hand and leads her into the cold, dark, empty church. Although, the girls aren't alone. Unexpectedly, there is a loud gunshot, and May drops to her knees. Dead. Cassandra then sees the hooded figure move forward, then darkness...

Kate

Shirenewton Primary School, Shirenewton

My Scary Dream

There was a man who was resting in bed. "Whooo!" he heard. He jumped up. He wasn't expecting it. The man went downstairs to investigate what it was. "Whoooooo!" There the noise was again. And suddenly, in the corner of his eye, he saw an open cupboard with a half-eaten cracker in it. The man turned away and he saw muddy footprints in the hall! "Whooooo!" There it was again. Suddenly, a door slammed! *What is happening to me?* the man thought. "Whooooo!" He saw the leaves rustle outside. He slowly opened his eyes... It was all just a dream!

George Tom Lobb Siddall (9)

Shirenewton Primary School, Shirenewton

Dino Island

Once a plane crashed on an island called Isla Bright. Only four people survived the crash! They didn't know dinos were alive! Then they went in the jungle and some velociraptors came. The people's names were Eli, Jeff, Jacub and Jerald. Jacub got killed by one of the raptors! The others ran as fast as they could. Then Eli found a radio! They contacted the military. They went back to the beach. The military came. Then suddenly a T-rex appeared! They ran to the military boats and left the island. The T-rex roared before the boat left far away.

George S (9)
Shirenewton Primary School, Shirenewton

Murder Doll

It was the coldest night of 1811 and all was silent. Well, all was silent until the village heard the deafening scream of Shyfly, the girl with no name. The suspicious murder was investigated. Let's go to the eleventh of August 1911, when Flur and her family moved in to The Lynx, a small bungalow with a big history. This is where the murder in 1811 took place!

One night, Flur heard a peculiar noise outside her bedroom. A noise she hadn't heard before. Suddenly, her bedroom door opened and she was shot! Was it manslaughter or murder...

Caitlin Morgan (10)
Shirenewton Primary School, Shirenewton

The Maze Of The Missing

The night was cold, dark and gloomy. Seven children were playing a game, but something did not seem right. There were only six people. They heard a scream and saw him! The murderer with the seventh child dead on the floor! The children ran into the house and another child was killed. They slammed the door shut and locked it, then through the window, they saw the murderer carrying dead bodies into the maze of the missing! The murderer was gone. They called the police and they went to investigate. They never returned. That maze is still there.

Evan D
Shirenewton Primary School, Shirenewton

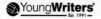

Toys In The Night

A girl, Ella, was sound asleep. Toys were everywhere! Everything was still in the night. Suddenly the clock struck midnight. One by one, Ella's toys came to life! They used some books to make a staircase to get up to Ella's bed. The racket woke Ella up! The toys leapt onto her and covered her until... Ella transformed! The toys had turned Ella into a toy! A polar bear toy in fact. The toys carried Ella under her bed, onto a blue slide and... *whoosh!*
Ella woke up the next morning as herself... but where were her toys?

Ella Parnell (9)

Shirenewton Primary School, Shirenewton

The Murderer In Disguise

It was a dark, gloomy night. A murder had just happened! The houses were grey, the sky was grey, the church was grey. Dan had just been murdered, but by who? Detective Eric and John tried to figure out the murder. They started by asking villagers to see what they had seen. Some said they had seen a hooded figure, others said they had seen a familiar face! Detective Eric said this was nonsense and they should move on, but the police got involved. Eric convinced them not to help. John got suspicious, then he realised Detective Eric did it!

Dylan Samuel Haddow (10)
Shirenewton Primary School, Shirenewton

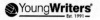

Stream

Once there was a girl called Ira and her dog Jupiter. Ira recently broke her arm and was walking Jupiter around the woods with her time off school. There had been rumours of a man who lives in the stream flowing through the woods. The man is a murderer. Ira ignored this and walked Jupiter. She was alone. Ira enjoyed hearing the sound of the water splash and the sticks crunch and footsteps. Wait, footsteps? She turned towards the stream to see a man tall and slender holding a knife! She tried to run but got dragged into the unknown...

Sienna Harford (11)
Shirenewton Primary School, Shirenewton

Ronaldo Got Stuck In A Chimney

Ronaldo was playing football. He was training for a match, Juventus vs Liverpool. He had to be fit for it. He loved playing football, this was his chance to shine. He kicked the ball so hard it went over the crossbar and it went in a chimney! He went to get it but he slipped and fell down the chimney. He got stuck and broke his leg! "Ouch!" he cried. "Oh I can't foul Salah!" He could not play. He was distraught. Dybala was very sad. Maducich, on the other hand, was happy because he could play up front.

Zak Baker (9)
Shirenewton Primary School, Shirenewton

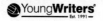

The Gaming Guy

One day when Fred was playing Roblox, he was on the fighting simulator. He got killed. He left the game and the power went out... He got sucked into the game. There was a message from Roblox saying 'Get out of the game in twenty-four hours or you will be trapped in Roblox forever. To get out, you need to complete obbys, tasks, finish simulators and get the best car in Bloxburg'. He started with the obbys, then the task, but he realized his twenty-four hours were nearly up! He needed to hurry up before time ran out...

Evan Walker
Shirenewton Primary School, Shirenewton

The Murder Mystery With The Mystical Unicorn

One sunny day Lilly went for a walk and came across a horse. As she was taking it home, she saw a ghost killer that looked like her long-lost brother! She went to bed and looked out of the window but instead of her horse, there was a beautiful unicorn that flew to her window.

"Get on my back and I'll show you something!"

A portal took them to a magical land of fairies! The Queen Fairy said that her brother got turned into a ghost killer by her husband who betrayed them. How will Lilly rescue her brother?

Martha Evelyn Garrett Lupo (8)

Shirenewton Primary School, Shirenewton

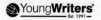
The Magic Football

It was a sunny day and people were playing football. Then a person called Jack said, "Don't play with that ball, it's dangerous!"
The boys ignored him and carried on playing with the ball. Jack couldn't take it so he picked the ball up and started to walk away. Suddenly a creepy face appeared on the ball and Jack threw it behind him! The ball hit one of the boys on the head and bit him! Suddenly the boys ran to their cars and the ball charged towards their cars. The boys just got away and fled.

Owen Read-Smith (9)
Shirenewton Primary School, Shirenewton

Mysterious Day

It was an ordinary day in the city centre of Newport. Dr Worth was looking for something to be dealt with. Dr Worth decided, as there was nothing to do, to go to the local café. Suddenly everyone was shouting! Someone stole all of the shop's money! Time for Dr Worth to save the day. Dr Worth started chasing the criminal! In a short space of time, Dr Worth was playing catch up. Dr Worth clung onto the criminal - he had an advantage as the criminal had the money in his hands. He got it! Dr Worth saved the day!

Alexander Duckworth (9)
Shirenewton Primary School, Shirenewton

Take Me To Church

One gloomy morning a girl called Faith went to church with her mother Janet. While saying her prayers, she was looking down but when she looked back up there was a creepy black cloak! Her mum couldn't see the cloak so Faith thought she wasn't alive but that was not true, she was still alive. As they were leaving the church, Faith saw the cloak again! After, she went closer to it. She saw it looked like a spirit, a bad one! Then she asked it a question. It didn't reply. Then the evil spirit stabbed her!

Phoebe Hine (10)
Shirenewton Primary School, Shirenewton

Lexy's Rainbow

Once in a faraway land lived a unicorn called Lexy and her animal friends. There was a rainbow that rained sweets but one day it stopped raining, so Lexy went to see what was wrong. Her animal friends were really worried so they said to Lexy, "Can we help you fix it?"
Lexy said, "Yes you can!"
So they went to ask the troll. It took a long time to get there because he lived on the other side of the forest but the troll was a nice troll. The troll helped and the rainbow was fixed!

Floelyn Lyra Skye Trim (10)
Shirenewton Primary School, Shirenewton

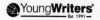

The Scarecrow

Sam is twenty-three years old and she lives by a church in Shirenewton. She owns a field and her best friend is a scarecrow called Grace.

One day Sam went to the beach, not knowing that something was going to happen. When she got home, she quickly went to bed. She looked out of her window and she was really confused because the scarecrow wasn't there! She didn't believe it. She thought she was just tired so she went to bed and checked it out in the morning. Grace wasn't there. She was sad.

Megan (10)

Shirenewton Primary School, Shirenewton

The Missing Unicorn

I was dreaming. I started to wake up. It was a Saturday. As I lifted my head off the pillow, I nearly had a heart attack! There in front of me was a unicorn!

She said to me, "Hello, I'm Lavender. I need to get back to my world. Can you help?"

I first thought, *nah, I'll never know how,* but I realised I knew how! I told her to stand on my book with a purple unicorn on and say her name. She did so, and as she did, she was sucked away! I was sad. "Bye!" I called.

Lauren Denné (9)
Shirenewton Primary School, Shirenewton

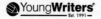
My Cat Is Missing

My cat is missing. Where to look? What to do? Where are you Misty? I looked in the wardrobe, looked in the bathtub? Where are you hiding? In the cupboard? No, you're not, where are you Misty? Where are you? Are you in the kitchen? No you're not, what to do? Are you in the attic? Where to look, what to do? Are you in the hallway or are you by the door? No, you're not, where are you? Are you next door? No, you're not. Come out wherever you are. There you are Misty! I missed you!

Isabel Bendall (9)
Shirenewton Primary School, Shirenewton

Enchanted Stallion

There was a girl called Maisie. She wanted to go out for a walk in the woods. She found a black stallion in the woods as soon as Maisie looked at the stallion, it disappeared! Scared, Maisie was screaming and she tripped over and broke her leg! The stallion cantered up to her and got Maisie onto his back. Maisie soon felt better after lying on his back. The stallion put Maisie to lie on two mushrooms but then a wolf came. The stallion raised up and fell on the wolf! Maisie got better.

Terah Rose Parkhouse (10)
Shirenewton Primary School, Shirenewton

The Night Of Mystery

It was a very misty night at Shirenewton church. It was ten o'clock in the evening. The vicar was packing up after the funeral of a butcher named Jeff. He was just putting the shovel away for the grave when he felt the wind or something. He turned around but there was nothing there. He felt it again! He turned around and the ghost of the butcher was standing there! Three hours later, it was morning. When people went to find him, he was lying in the butcher's grave... Dead.

Ethan B
Shirenewton Primary School, Shirenewton

Saving Superhero

In a dark chilly gloom, a lamp post flickered. A young girl named Emily looked around the corner. Emily was a clever superhero who had a big mission to save The Shard. Mr Ozard was going to fly an aeroplane into it! That was not her only problem, Emily was a teacher who taught maths so she had to go out at night. So one night she went to The Shard and saw Mr Ozard! She caught him in a huge rope and bought him to the police. Her job was a lot easier and she enjoyed it so much.

Seren Burston-Yates (9)
Shirenewton Primary School, Shirenewton

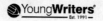

The Cat Of Ancient Egypt

I finally got there, ancient Egypt. It was a very weird place with pyramids. Then I saw the Egyptians! So I went up to them and they taught to me their ways. I went exploring in the pyramids but I got lost in one of the pyramids! Then out of nowhere, I saw a pharaoh! He picked me up and then said, "Are you lost?"

I nodded. He showed me the way out and I just stayed with him. In the end, I became his pet. I lived in ancient Egypt and never ever wanted to leave!

Demi Morgan
Shirenewton Primary School, Shirenewton

The Adventures Of A Villain!

Once there lived an evil mister called Indistrucktable Ian. Where did he live you say? He lived in a peculiar place underground. Give me a break, how weird is that? He was evil all his life. When he was in his fifties he thought, *aha that's it, I'm going to release a giant bot of me into the world!* Then he did just that. He released it. No one could stop him! They had to obey his rules for the rest of their lives and couldn't do anything else.

Aiden Carpenter

Shirenewton Primary School, Shirenewton

The Back Way Road

In the beginning, there was just a forest. In the forest was a human. The human was Stewart. Stewart had grey eyes and black hair and he was all alone; he had no one apart from his father who was lying in a pool of blood. Stewart had sworn revenge as he found his father dead. All he knew was that his father was dead and he hoped to avenge him, so he went to find his killer. It was a zombie! Stewart ran. Luckily for him he did not see it attack but he did feel it!

Evan F
Shirenewton Primary School, Shirenewton

Into The Game

Hi, I"m Jamey. I'm eleven. I"ll start at the start. First, I found a board game in the park in the morning. Then I was in a vast jungle and a panther was pouncing towards me, so I dodged it and started to run! Then I found myself in a desert with a stampede of triceratops coming for me! I braced but they never came. Then I was by the board game I saw this morning and a note was on it. 'Roll a six to win'. So I rolled a six and I woke up!

Barnaby Hitchcock (10)
Shirenewton Primary School, Shirenewton

Eating Xmas On Xmas Eve

One cold night when Santa was making gifts, he had a plan to make Xmas no more! He had a team of elves planning to eat the Xmas spirit on Xmas eve! The next day an elf was planning to stop Santa and the ten elves, but the elf needed twenty more elves. It would be hard work for one elf! So he did. He made a vow to the elves in Lapland in the North Pole. They came the very next day! First came Fred, Samuel and Thomas. They got straight to work...

Thomas Burbidge (9)
Shirenewton Primary School, Shirenewton

Dead And Gone

One misty day in Shirenewton there was a man called Tom. He was a lonely man. There was a girl and her name was Kate. She was very lonely so she went on a walk down to the woods to shoot birds. Then Tom shot a bird! The bird fell on the ground. Then he shot a bullet but it hit Kate in the heart! Blood went on her clothes and shoes. There was a scream! Tom ran and screamed. Kate was dead. Tom ran away...

Dylan Morgan Poole (10)
Shirenewton Primary School, Shirenewton

The Mirror

Once there were two boys called Luke and Max. One day they found an abandoned house. "What do you think that is?" commented Luke, knowing exactly what it was.

"Don't know!" wondered Max. "Let's check it out!" As they tiptoed into the derelict house, they realised the broken, rusting windows which silently cracked, creating a ghostly atmosphere. The ceiling above them creaked like someone was up there. Luke came to an old small room. When he found his way to the back of the room, he came across an old mirror. He looked in it and it changed his life...

George Evans (10)
St Edward's RC Primary School, Lees

Demon Headteacher

Early one morning in St Edward's School, the demon headteacher was searching for footballs. Mr McMahon bellowed, "Where are those annoying footballs?"

Then he immediately threw ferocious fireballs at them! Footballs were flying everywhere! Children and teachers were running into their classrooms, frightened and scared. Mrs Loach even called the police and fire brigade! Mr McMahon was angry because the police had arrived and warned him of the dangers. Everyone in school was terrified because of the incident. So now the demon headteacher Mr McMahon could control his powers and their school would be safe forever.

Bella Brennan (7)
St Edward's RC Primary School, Lees

Love To Another World

"Whoaah!" Daisy dragged me ferociously towards the bush. She barked frantically. A shimmer blinded me... Woken by Daisy whimpering, I overheard cruel owners shouting at their dogs. This planet needed kindness! Calling over a dog, Daisy pawed his frozen heart. He'd obviously never been shown affection! His heart glowed pink and he immediately spread cheer amongst his friends. Suddenly, the warmth exhausted me. *Zzzz!* I woke with a start back at home. *Was I dreaming? Wait, a dog collar!* I shook it and it glowed with pink hearts, just like the dogs. I felt confused but happy. We spread love!

Ellie-Beth Power (8)

St Edward's RC Primary School, Lees

The Cave Of Doom

Two friends wanted to do something more exciting than just get out of bed, go to school and return to bed. They wanted adventure. They embarked on a cave expedition. It was tough. The cave floor grazed their knees. The water half-drowned them! Lost and in desperation, they turned back, each day pulling themselves through the cave. They were too exhausted even to speak. They slept sporadically. Suddenly, *boom!* They both screamed as they tumbled through the freshly-created sinkholes in the cave. Generations after, people still come to pay their respects. The legend of The Cave of Doom lives on.

Ciara Postlethwaite (10)
St Edward's RC Primary School, Lees

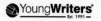
The Micromice

Tilly raced to the library. She searched for her contents and came across a letter. It read 'Anybody trustworthy, please help save the micromice before it's too late! Signed, Captain J.'. She thought, *what on Earth could a micromouse be?* Suddenly, she landed on a rocky path! She looked around and found small creatures crawling around in a cage. They had devilish red eyes! So that's what the letter meant! She was sent to help the micromice. She pulled the cage as hard as she could. Unfortunately, she became trapped too! Then a dark figure appeared...

Eavan Malunga (10)
St Edward's RC Primary School, Lees

Different Dimensions

One sunny day in a deserted village in West California there lived a thirteen-year-old boy called Jake. He was a superior agent who was on a discreet mission because he was a double agent trying to save and conquer the universe! He came across multiple aliens trying to overthrow Zephael, who was trying to reign havoc on Planet Earth. Zephael was a three-headed beast who brainwashed people! Jake had to impersonate Zephael's alien guards to destroy Zephael's brainwashing machine and free the human race! The next day, Jake received another world-ending case...

Yvonne Mwangi (10)
St Edward's RC Primary School, Lees

The Magical Rainforest

Last night I was in an exciting dream. I was in a beautiful green rainforest. There was an enormous elephant, a terrifying tiger, a mischievous monkey and a ginormous giraffe! When the elephant sprayed water into the sky, a bright rainbow appeared. The tiger looked amazing because it had a huge pattern all over its body! The giraffe was so tall that I could see the whole world from clinging to its neck. The monkey had grabbed a bunch of bananas from a tree! *What a wonderful place this would be to live with all these amazing animals and creatures...*

Amelia Grace Riley (7)
St Edward's RC Primary School, Lees

The Passage Through The Cellar Door

Slowly I lifted my head from my pillow. Everything looked the same but felt different. I walked downstairs. I saw markings on the walls! Slowly a door opened on its own! I looked more closely at the door. I saw deep scratch marks over it. Suddenly I noticed it was a cellar door! Silently I crept inside. Immediately I was in a completely different place where shadows were creeping about! I turned to walk back through the door but it had disappeared! The shadows started to look quite lifelike. *Now I am stuck here forever with the creepy ghosts...*

Carys Evans (9)
St Edward's RC Primary School, Lees

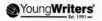

Icelantic

As soon as I stepped through the portal, I felt a breeze of chills. Where could I be? Spain? Greenland? Suddenly a girl wearing silky clothes passed by. I had so many questions that needed to be answered. In the corner of my eye, I saw a sign that said, *Welcome to Icelantic!* Out of nowhere, I saw two red polar bears! I gasped in amazement, then realised there were thousands of them surrounding the iceberg! People were building places to sleep for the night an red polar bears found places to rest. It was an extraordinary place to live!

Rebecca Norton (10)
St Edward's RC Primary School, Lees

The Nature Walk

Hi, I'm Lucy. I own a pet rescue centre. Today we went on a nature walk. Five children came and we went on a special adventure! We needed to find insects and tick them off our lists. Ladybirds, dragonflies, frogs and tadpoles. The children arrived and were ready for the walk. Suddenly, the children saw a puppy. One said, "I think she is lost, we should take her with us until the owner is found!"

"But first, let's take her on our adventure walk!"

"Let's call her Snowflake," said a little boy.

Annabelle Dervan (9)
St Edward's RC Primary School, Lees

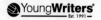

The Mythical Letter

One day a girl called Ella lived far away in the snowy mountains. The girl received a letter from a mysterious person. Inside the envelope was a treasure map! Ella decided to follow the map. It led her to a dark, gloomy forest. Dawn soon fell and Ella fell asleep lying on the leafy ground. In the morning, she was woken by a strange sound. Ella went to explore and was amazed to see a centaur walking by! All of a sudden she heard someone shout, "Breakfast is ready!"
This made her think. Was it all just a dream?

Ella Barlow (9)
St Edward's RC Primary School, Lees

The Monster

Teachers make people tidy up but what would happen if they didn't? Sometimes one would chat, then the whole class would get louder and louder until they are shouting at each other. Today, they did that. "If you do that again, I will turn green and grow horns!" exclaimed the teacher. The class became quieter. Soon, they were loud again! This time she really took her word for it. Then she slipped on a banana peel and flattened 267 people! Then the building fell and flattened her! She was put in the museum. Everyone was relieved.

Alannah Ashton (8)
St Edward's RC Primary School, Lees

Jungle Mania

One day Sam and Oliver were in the Amazon being chased by a bear! They climbed into a boat and sailed away. Then they got off and walked into the main section of the jungle. After walking around, they saw a lonely cottage with cobwebbed windows and a red door. Oliver said to go and explore it so they did. They opened the door and crept inside. They searched the top and found nothing. Then they went into the basement. When they searched the basement, Oliver strangely went missing! Oliver was never seen again to this day.

Sam Leach (10)
St Edward's RC Primary School, Lees

Dear Diary

Yesterday was eventful. In the morning I woke up, ate my usual breakfast of ashes and coffee and I heard the news that a new princess was in town. Being a dragon, I needed to kidnap her! It's my job, of course. You see, I'm amazing at capturing people, especially princesses. I have been practising all my life! In the middle of the night, I set off to kidnap her. She was easy to kidnap! I picked her up and flew her back to my castle. Suddenly, Prince Charming grabbed my leg! He took back the new princess.

Emily Richmond (10)
St Edward's RC Primary School, Lees

UFO On Earth With A Bump

One day two people were on their way to the moon in a rocket. As soon as they reached the moon, they saw two green dots. They discovered it was a little alien out of a hole! As they saw it, it ran away. When they looked up, they saw a UFO! They ran but it sucked them up and took them to Earth and dropped them down. They had handshakes with aliens! Then they got taken to hospital. They heard a *whoosh* over the hospital. "B-bob-bop!" said the aliens...

Rory Nield (8)
St Edward's RC Primary School, Lees

The Forest Wolf

As I crept into the forest I could hear freaky noises. I fell over a branch and quickly jumped up. Out of nowhere, a savage wolf started to chase me! I ran for miles and miles. I was terrified. I finally got away through the trees but sadly my shoes sank into some sloppy gooey mud. I was tired so I went into a little hut. Guess who was in there? It was the furious, hideous wolf! So I ran and ran until my legs could run no more. I ran all the way back home!

Olly Maher (9)
St Edward's RC Primary School, Lees

The Candyland People

Emma, Emily and Bella were swimming in the golden ocean to the mermaids and huge Merpup hotel. Emma and Emily are my pet merpups. When we were there, there were not a lot of mermaids and the hotel was almost empty.

During check-in, all the mermaids went from gloomy to happy, "Yay, you are here!" shouted everybody.

"Why are you so excited?" replied Emma and Bella.

"Don't you know?" said Max.

"No, what's wrong?" they urged.

"The Candyland people are back!" exclaimed Max.

"Oh no!" they yelled.

The Candyland people were coming to steal all the mermaids...

Jamie McKeith (9)
St Joseph's Convent School For Girls, Wanstead

The Mermaids

The naughty mermaids stole the pearl of life and the helpful mermaids tried to get the pearl of life back, but the helpful mermaids couldn't take the pearl of life because they couldn't get through the naughty mermaids' guards!

"What shall we do?" asked the youngest mermaids.

"Why don't we go behind them and then we slip into the space over there?" asked the younger mermaid.

"Okay, let's do that," said the older mermaid.

So when they saw the naughty mermaids, they began to fight! Then the naughty mermaids lost and the helpful mermaids won.

Samantha Sawyerr (7)
St Joseph's Convent School For Girls, Wanstead

Pearl Of Life

One minute I was in a white room, then I was under the deep blue sea with a tail! Mermaids surrounded me calling "Oceana!" Where was I? The sound got louder. I heard them saying, "Where's the pearl!" Then they stated, "We need you to find the pearl!" We travelled to the desert. As I climbed out of the sea, it felt like the hot sand was eating me up.

When I finally got up, my tail disappeared as quick as a flash! We saw the bunny-like crabs. They shouted, "Fight!"

The mermaids cried, "Get out your swords, fight..."

Maria Bedneau (8)
St Joseph's Convent School For Girls, Wanstead

Were Mermaids Real?

It was a myth, it was a legend but I knew something, it was true! Were mermaids real? Yes, I thought to myself. I felt a chill go down my spine as I looked at the crashing waves and tumbling rocks. Suddenly I saw a tail! Was it true? Were mermaids real? The next night I asked my parents. "No," was my mother's reply. "You're thinking silly things, surely it was a narwhal or a dolphin or even a whale? Mermaids aren't real!" my mother scolded me.

Her logical answer made me feel ignorant. Was it true? Was I right?

Zahra Nisar (8)
St Joseph's Convent School For Girls, Wanstead

Candy Land

I was in Candyland, strolling through the candy woods with my friend Strawberry and Lic-Lic her pet bunny who talked gibberish. I was licking the leaves and eating the delicious, smooth trees. I asked Strawberry if she had family nearby. She said, "Yes, let's go!" and she pulled me off to town. There was a house made out of gingerbread. I just wanted to gobble it all up but I would not be a very good friend to Strawberry. Desperately, I rang the doorbell after I licked my finger - mmm, yummy. "Are your parents home, Strawberry?"

Olivia Day
St Joseph's Convent School For Girls, Wanstead

Petunia

On a dark, gloomy night, I was checking my new doll, Petunia. I picked her up and ran my fingers through her glossy hair. Surprisingly, her eyes flickered! She bared her vast, red eyes. I was petrified, my blood pressure zoomed high! I screamed, but no sound came out. I tried to calm myself down. I did, until her thin, slender legs automatically started to move! Only God knows how it all happened. Droplets of sweat came running down my forehead, I hoped it was a dream! I spun around in a gargantuan hurry, and I awoke, under my covers!

Micheala Hagan (9)
St Joseph's Convent School For Girls, Wanstead

Mako Mermaids

The mermaids are on Mako Island, Zac is in the tunnel. He sees a light! Shaking, he slowly goes towards it and touches the shining, yellow light. Suddenly, he falls through the floor, it opens up like a sand timer! Zac ends up in the moon pool where the mermaids are. The mermaids swim as fast as they can with Zac in their arms. They can only swim up to the shore, they have to leave him on the beach.

He wakes up two hours later, cold. He's amazed to see he has become a merman! What will happen next?

Tiana John-Rose (8)
St Joseph's Convent School For Girls, Wanstead

Trapped

Bella was walking on the beach when she suddenly saw her friend calling her. She jumped into the water. The water spat out all the seaweed onto her. When she finally got in, she realised all her friends were trapped! As quick as a flash she realised who was behind it, Merman Black. Suddenly another trap fell but it was too late. "Merman black is at it again," said Bella. He started swimming fast but Bella was faster because of her powers! She now knew what he was after, the diamond of life...

Maya Malik (9)
St Joseph's Convent School For Girls, Wanstead

Frozen

Three best friends, Eliot, Lui and Benjamin were playing outside in the garden. Suddenly, something appeared out of the shadows. They were running at their top speed. They ran for their lives! Eliot and Benjamin were chased. They were panting for breath. They were trapped and instantly froze on the spot. How can they be free? Suddenly their fourth friend joined them and asked if he could play 'Stuck in the Mud'. So they became free and restarted the game. Run for your lives...

Anna Gillert (7)
St Joseph's Convent School For Girls, Wanstead

Jimmy And The Asleta

Once upon a time, there was a person called Jimmy. He was on a boat sailing to an island in the middle of the Atlantic Ocean. When he got there he saw a weird-looking animal. It talked like a human. It looked really cool.

"What are you?" Jimmy said.

The animal said, "I'm an Asleta."

"That's a weird name for an animal," said Jimmy.

Jimmy brought the Asleta home, back to his house. He called it Duffy. Duffy really liked going on walks. Jimmy would take Duffy on a walk five times a day and they lived happily ever after.

Lewis Cameron King (10)
Strathpeffer Primary School, Strathpeffer

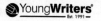

Legendary Planet

Grace woke up and looked around her. Before she could say anything, something rustled inside the bushes. A furry type creature jumped out! Grace put out a hand to pet it but it scampered away. She followed it. She pushed past all the bushes and there were animals everywhere! They were legendary and Grace had been sure they didn't exist. They came over to her and she knelt down to pet them. They were really soft. The little furry creature followed Grace as she kept exploring. There was a beautiful flowing waterfall with fish jumping. Was it a dream?

Grace Grant (10)
Strathpeffer Primary School, Strathpeffer

Lazerman Vs Evilman

Once upon a time, a superhero called Lazerman could shoot lasers out of his hands and head. He could also fly with his boots. He was in a city and he was there to protect it from an evil supervillain called Evilman. Evilman could also fly and he was super strong! One day when Lazerman was protecting the city, Evilman showed up and he wanted to do a battle with Lazerman! Evilman punched Lazerman in the chest which sent him crashing into buildings that destroyed the city! Then Lazerman shot lasers that killed Evilman and Lazerman saved the day!

Harvey Wright (11)
Strathpeffer Primary School, Strathpeffer

The Unexpected Letter

Charlotte heard the postman drop the letters at the red letterbox and walked to the door. There was only one letter, addressed to her. She ran to her room and greedily ripped open the envelope. This is what it said: 'Dear Charlotte, you have been selected for the secret spy association academy. Please get parental consent and we will send another letter for more details'. Charlotte sprinted downstairs and told her dad. Her dad wheeled over to her in his rusty wheelchair and adjusted his glasses. He read the note and gave her a bear hug!

Oona Macdonald (10)
Strathpeffer Primary School, Strathpeffer

The Adventure

Frizz went through the portal. He saw a volcano and it was exploding! Rocks were launching at him. He was so scared. He saw this weird-looking portal and walked through. Everything looked upside-down. He was dashing down the room and suddenly he was in a black room. It had no windows or doors but he saw a hatch and jumped through. He saw his friend and saved him from the monster! Suddenly, bang! The monster chased them so they belted it through the door, rocks and molten lava launching at them! They had found their way home.

Kayden Aird (10)
Strathpeffer Primary School, Strathpeffer

The Invisible Man!

The invisible man arrived at the dark forest. It was pitch-black. He couldn't see a thing. Luckily he brought a torch. Then suddenly he heard a loud bang. He dropped his torch and ran. Then he remembered he was invisible! Then he slipped and fell into a pond. He didn't like it here. And he ran again. Finally he realised there was no escape. He wanted to go home badly. Suddenly he heard a voice shouting, "Go away, go away, go away!" So he ran and ran, never to be seen again and not discovering anything new!

Lena Jean Butler-Whittaker (9)
Strathpeffer Primary School, Strathpeffer

Breadisd And The Time Machine

Breadisd was walking through the woods and heard a loud crash. "What was that?" said Breadisd.

He went to go see what it was. "It's a time machine," said Breadisd. He took it back to his house to fix it. After two hours, he got it. "Yeah!" said Breadisd. He got inside it. "I'm going to the year 2245!" said Breadisd.

He went forward in time and ended up in a chicken coop. Suddenly a big guy walked in and told Breadisd to watch out. He walked out and saw a monster! He returned to 2019 and destroyed the machine.

Ieuan Hedges (10)
Strathpeffer Primary School, Strathpeffer

Clark And Puppy Wuppy's Death Day

One Halloween night it was time to go guising but not for everyone. It's time to meet Clark and Puppy Wuppy or PW for short. They never go guising because that is the day they died. Yes, they are ghosts! Clark and PW have never left the graveyard and no kid has gone to the graveyard on Halloween night.

Tonight, PW and Clark were feeling brave. So, that night they left the graveyard and went guising! They had so much fun and they made a lot of friends.

From now on they love Halloween and every day of the year!

Charlotte Frame (10)
Strathpeffer Primary School, Strathpeffer

The Mystery Robber!

One dark and stormy night a man named Collin crept into the jeweller's tower. I thought to myself, *what is he doing? He isn't a guard or anything.* He came out with a beautiful necklace! I thought for a moment he had stolen it! I rang the police and put the stealing siren off in the tower. I could hear another siren, it was the police! I was so glad. They took him away and they gave me the necklace as my reward! I was so incredibly happy. Two years later and he is still in jail, wooo!

Charlotte Rose (9)
Strathpeffer Primary School, Strathpeffer

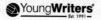

Lucy's Lucky Day!

So one day there was a girl called Lucy. She was a good gymnast and I mean really good. She was going to a competition so she was getting ready for it.

She got in the car and she drove to the competition in Strathpeffer. She got to Strathpeffer. She was at the competition venue. First she had floor and then she had beam and then she had bars! Then it was time to announce the winners. On beam, she came first! On bars she came first and on floor, she came first. That was a fantastic day.

Cody Mackenzie (10)
Strathpeffer Primary School, Strathpeffer

Detective Charlotte

It was a dark and stormy night and a little girl called Sophie was just put to bed. Her window was open and in the morning, Sophie was gone! So her parents called Detective Charlotte. When she got there she found footprints of mud. They followed the footprints which led into the woods! Detective Charlotte found a sack but no one was in it. She found some food prints of pizza. She followed it! It led to an old scary house. She found Sophie all alone and she took her back to her house!

Lara Maree Rasdale (10)
Strathpeffer Primary School, Strathpeffer

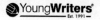
The Time Machine

Mia was playing outside. Then Mia spotted a time machine! Mia jumped in it and spilt orange juice all over it and it turned on. *Bang!* She was in the future! There were loads of flying cars and robots. She met a pizza robot. It was funny. Mia went to the top of the Mountain of Future! It was beautiful but it was time to go home. So she went back home by spilling more orange juice on the computer. When Mia got home she hid the time machine and went out and played football.

Ella Cormack (10)
Strathpeffer Primary School, Strathpeffer

Super Dog

In the city there was a Super Dog. He saved people but people didn't talk to him. Other dogs ran after Super Dog to get him to save dogs instead of people.

On the weekends, Super Dog went to his favourite place to eat there. He loved it so much because his favourite food was there and his favourite food was very nice dog food! After he had his dog food, he decided to save other dogs. So he flew around the city to find dogs in trouble. After that, they all spoke to Super Dog.

Isla Stewart (10)
Strathpeffer Primary School, Strathpeffer

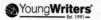

Tim's Terrifying Story!

One day Tim took a submarine from a shop and he drove it into the sea until he went to the bottom of the Atlantic Ocean. Then he got his claw from the bottom of his submarine and he grabbed an innocent fish to eat at home. Next, he could see a treasure chest so he grabbed it with the claw and he opened it and it was filled with gold! Suddenly a giant shark went to attack his submarine so he drove it back to shore! After that, he went back home and ate the big tasty fish!

Fraser James Wright (11)
Strathpeffer Primary School, Strathpeffer

The Old House Mystery!

We started unpacking our stuff from the big lorry. We had been driving for hours to England. We got some stuff set up and went to bed. *Creak creak!* I woke up with with the noise of floorboards creaking and noises coming from the attic! I grabbed the magnifying glass and put my slippers on and slowly crept out of my room. I could hear snoring coming from my mum and dad's room. I slowly crept down the stairs and saw a floating sheet heading to the attic...

Teagen Syrjanen (10)
Strathpeffer Primary School, Strathpeffer

The Record Climb

Hi, my name is Fraser and this is my friend
Alasdair. We both love to climb.
We are going for a record climb of ten hours by
climbing El Capitan and Mont Fear. If we do it, we
will hold the world record and I will probably sleep
for ages afterwards! We have been practising for
two years and tomorrow, at dawn, we will start to
climb El Capitan then Mont Fear. Hopefully, we do
it and we will get the Guinness World Record,
maybe a knighting! Will we do it?

Fraser Alick Morrison (10)
Strathpeffer Primary School, Strathpeffer

Zombies

A man went into a hall and got stuck in the hall. So he tried to get out with his Katana sword. It didn't work, so he tried to get out with his axe but it did not work and zombies started to come in! His friends came in too so they killed all the zombies but more came in! They ran to the resort room and tried to get out through the roof. They sent Barry up to the roof. Barry made it and got out! The friends came up too and they shouted, "Yay, yay!"

Craig Stewart (10)
Strathpeffer Primary School, Strathpeffer

Ghost Cookie

It was a nice day in Cookie Land but the evil ghost cookie was there. He robbed the bank! Then he ran and ran and ran. The poor cookie was in bad pain. Then he saw a big bear and he said a magic spell. The spell goes 'La, la, moo, moo'. The spell worked! The poor cookie died of happiness. The poor ghost cookie fell into the pond and that was the end of the very, very bad ghost cookie. He dissolved in the pond and he was never seen again.

Katie Campbell (10)
Strathpeffer Primary School, Strathpeffer

Consequences

He walked through the forest, encountering a strange old man. The man offered a chess game. He accepted. Nearby there were some cities. Eventually, they finished. He stood up to leave. The old man said, "The man with no nose is coming for you!" He got home to find the world was destroyed. He stood there thinking. Did he do this? That's what he was going to find out, no matter the consequences...

Kai Condon (10)
Strathpeffer Primary School, Strathpeffer

In The Woods

In the woods lay a deadly wolf. He killed twenty people in a single day. It was a legendary story but it was true. People did not believe in it but one day, the wolf was seen in the woods near their homes! The wolf ran after them and he killed them. One got away! The one who got away told the story of The Legend Deadly Wolf...

Ali Taylor (9)
Strathpeffer Primary School, Strathpeffer

Garry, The Disco Ghost!

One day an ancient explorer wanted to get close up to the face of the moon. Barry the explorer set off in Apollo 11 to space! He started to hum a melancholy tune, thinking he might never return. Barry settled into space, before bouncing like a gazelle onto the moon! He leapt to the face, then Molly Moon asked him, "Do you know the planet Pluto?"

"Yes, I do?"

"Well then, go there!"

"Okay."

Barry set off to Pluto and met a ghost called Garry! Garry was a disco ghost and had a disco hat! *A new species!* Barry thought.

Imogen Cobner-Vale (9)
Wootton St Peter's CE Primary School, Wootton Village

The Gem Girls

Not too long ago, there were four girls named Emerald, Amethyst, Garnet and Sapphire. They were best friends because of something Sapphire noticed: they were all named after gems! Anyway, they were sixteen at the time. They all went camping in the Amazon. They were so excited. On the way, they couldn't stop talking about it. When they finally got there, they set up their tent in a clearing. They had so much fun but night-time was petrifying! They heard millions of noises. They were overjoyed when they woke up. Then they saw Amethyst completely dead...

Harriet Emily Johnson (10)
Wootton St Peter's CE Primary School, Wootton Village

The Briefcase

There was a town called Wootton but one day a girl came. She changed everything. The girl's name was Rose. She was staying in a hotel and she was carrying a briefcase. She went to her room and stepped inside. A girl stepped in behind her. There was another cool world! There were lots of creatures. Rose was playing with a creature, his name was Mister Monrow. The other girl said, "Can I play?"

Rose said, "Of course! What is your name?"

The girl said, "Sienna!"

Rose said, "Well, let's play!"

Rose Kyarra Stevens (9)
Wootton St Peter's CE Primary School, Wootton Village

Amelia's Adventure In Spain

Amelia woke to the sun shining through her window. For a moment, she forgot where she was. "I'm in Spain!" she exclaimed. After breakfast, Amelia and her family walked to the harbour for a boat trip to explore an island. Just as they approached the island, something blew into Amelia's face! It was a map! The map looked just like the island. Amelia followed the map to rocks marked with a spade symbol. Amelia dug up a chest. Inside the chest was Christopher Columbus' exploration diary! On the last page of his diary was another map. Where would it lead?

Bethany Rose (8)
Wootton St Peter's CE Primary School, Wootton Village

Heroes Of War

Welcome to Evoka, a place of high technology but a place at war with the Arkanians. This solar system is in the Milky Way but a thousand lightyears away. The solar system of Ira consists of three planets, Evoka, Arka and Ieka. This is how it all began. Commander Axer from Ieka came. He said he needed them to attack a planet outside of the solar system but actually he was asking them to attack Arka! They arrived. The battle weakened both sides. Arka lost important buildings! Evoka lost troops! Ieka had done it! They could take over both planets.

Charlie Cooke (10)
Wootton St Peter's CE Primary School, Wootton Village

Treasure Pirate

I walked off my island to find an abandoned ship. I walked towards the ship and found a box inside. It was a treasure map! I sailed the ship and followed the map. It took me to a family of great white sharks who were protecting the treasure. I jumped in dipping and diving the sharks! I reached the treasure and found a glowing red stone! I picked it up. Suddenly, all the sharks stopped swimming. They looked at me. Whoever holds the stone holds the power to the underwater kingdom! I now hold the power to the underwater kingdom forever.

Maria Catalina (7)
Wootton St Peter's CE Primary School, Wootton Village

Impershmae!

What a peculiar thing I saw. Nobody believes me! Here's the story. Yesterday evening when it was snowing, I went into the woods and heard a strange sound. Obviously I had to check it out. You will never guess what I saw! An Impershmae! It was just like I was dreaming. Suddenly, it scampered over to the oak tree and then it pulled out a shiny golden key! It shoved it into the trunk and open sesame! It was gone for a very long time but when it came out, loads of creatures followed it out! They ended up partying!

Ruby Gillett (9)
Wootton St Peter's CE Primary School, Wootton Village

YOUNG WRITERS INFORMATION

We hope you have enjoyed reading this book – and that you will continue to in the coming years.

If you're a young writer who enjoys reading and creative writing, or the parent of an enthusiastic poet or story writer, do visit our website **www.youngwriters.co.uk**. Here you will find free competitions, workshops and games, as well as recommended reads, a poetry glossary and our blog. There's lots to keep budding writers motivated to write!

If you would like to order further copies of this book, or any of our other titles, then please give us a call or order via your online account.

Young Writers
Remus House
Coltsfoot Drive
Peterborough
PE2 9BF
(01733) 890066
info@youngwriters.co.uk

Join in the conversation!
Tips, news, giveaways and much more!

 YoungWritersUK   **@YoungWritersCW**